First Person History

Washington's Crossing

By

Adam Zimmerman, Sr

Copyright © 2024 by Adam Zimmerman, Sr

All rights reserved.

No part of this book may be reproduced, stored in a retrieval system, or transmitted in any form or by any means—electronic, mechanical, photocopying, recording, or otherwise—without the prior written permission of the author, except as permitted by U.S. copyright law.

For permission requests, contact the author at adam.zimmerman@hotmail.com.

Independently published.

ISBN: 9798784819826

This is a work of fiction. Names, characters, places, and incidents either are the product of the author's imagination or are used fictitiously. Any resemblance to actual persons, living or dead, events, or locales is entirely coincidental.

First Edition

Dedication:
To my children, Austin and AJ.
You were my inspiration for this book.
To my wife Danielle, for her love and support.

Chapter One

They wandered the empty hallway of their elementary school, suddenly aware of how quiet it was without dozens of other kids around them. The only sound was the squeaking of their sneakers on the tile floor.

"Are you sure Mrs. Thompson wanted us to meet her here at 8:00 pm?" Charlie asked his friend skeptically. Austin thought he was sure, but the more he thought about it, the more he questioned himself. The front doors of the school were locked when they got there. They had to walk around the building and finally found a side door that was unlocked. It led them into a wing of the building that they had never been in before, and both boys had attended William G. Jones Elementary since kindergarten.

"Well, I thought so," Austin replied. "Maybe she meant tomorrow morning at 8:00 am, instead." Charlie looked at his friend and rolled his eyes. As they continued walking down the long hallway, Charlie was about to tell Austin that they should turn around and head home, when he noticed something odd. The hallway they were walking through looked abandoned. There were no posters on the walls, no class schedules on the bulletin boards, nothing around them to indicate that children had used this hallway or the classrooms recently. In fact, the whole place smelled musty and there were cobwebs everywhere.

"What is this place?" Austin asked as they walked past a rusty drinking fountain. "It looks like nobody's been here in a hundred years. How old is our school, anyway?"

"I don't know, but it's probably fifty years old, at least," Charlie replied. He knew that Jones Elementary was one of the oldest school buildings in the district, but not much else about it.

"I'm pretty sure Mrs. Thompson isn't here," said Charlie. "Let's get out of here, this place is giving me the creeps." Charlie turned around and started heading back toward the door, but Austin spotted something ahead of them that he wanted to investigate.

"Hang on a minute. Come look at this," Austin called to his friend.

Austin and Charlie had been best friends for as long as they could remember. They grew up just around the corner from each other in a nice, quiet neighborhood a short walk from their school. Austin was 12 years old and was a natural athlete. He was already the best player on their city league baseball team, even though the team included junior high schoolers as well. Austin was bigger than most of his peers in the 6th grade. He did alright in school but didn't really enjoy it. His dream was to be a big-league ballplayer, or if that didn't work out, join the Marines. Charlie, on the other hand, was one of the smallest kids in his class, and one of the youngest at 11 years old. He was also one of the smartest. Kids at school called Charlie a bookworm, but he didn't mind the name. He loved reading and couldn't figure out why other kids didn't enjoy it as much as he did. He especially loved how reading could transport you to another place and time, and let you experience things that you could never experience in real life.

Charlie turned back around and walked to where Austin was now standing. Austin was looking at a row of lockers on the right side of the hallway. The lockers didn't look like the tiny half-lockers the boys used for their books and backpacks. These lockers were larger and looked much older. Instead of combination locks built into the locker as theirs had, these lockers had a small handle that slid up and down, with a hole in it to attach a lock. In the center of the row of lockers, there was one locker wrapped in yellow caution tape. There was a handwritten sign on yellow, faded notebook paper that read "Danger - Do Not Open" taped to the outside of the locker.

"What do you make of this?" Austin asked Charlie as they stood shoulder-to-shoulder staring at their discovery. As Charlie examined the locker closer, he noticed that the caution tape had been ripped, almost as if the locker had been opened recently. Then he noticed that there was a lock hanging from the handle.

"It's locked," Charlie replied, still staring at the locker, "but it looks like someone tried to open it. Or someone opened it, and then locked it again." Austin, noticing the lock for the first time, reached out and nonchalantly gave it a tug downward. To his surprise, the lock disengaged and popped open. Austin withdrew his hand as if he'd been bitten by a snake. Both boys took a step backward.

"Whoa, I wasn't expecting that," Austin said. "Should we open it?"

"I don't think so. Somebody wanted it to stay closed," Charlie said. "Come on, it's getting late. I still have homework to do." Austin wasn't satisfied.

"Where's your sense of adventure? What's the worst thing that could be in there? Some smelly gym socks from 1982? Some overdue math homework?" Austin looked at the number at the top of the locker. It read 419.

"Fine. A quick peek inside and then we need to leave," Charlie relented. Austin reached for the open lock and removed it from the handle. Then he lifted the handle and slowly opened the locker, expecting anything and nothing at the same time.

Chapter Two

As he slowly opened the locker door, Austin found himself hoping they would find something interesting. When the door was finally open, his eyes searched the darkness but found nothing. It was empty.

"Bummer," Austin said as he began to close the locker again.

"Wait, what's that?" Charlie said, pointing to the top shelf of the locker. It was too high for him to reach, but it was just above the top of Austin's head. He looked up at it.

"It looks like a book. Like a schoolbook," Austin said as he reached for the item. He removed it from the locker shelf and the boys inspected it. It was indeed a book. A very old, very heavy book. It was covered in a film of dust so thick that it completely blocked out the name of the book. In the thick dust, Austin could clearly make out a set of fingerprints, like the book had been picked up recently. He wiped the dust from the cover and read the title, *First Person History*.

"Cool, I love history. I wonder how old this is?" Charlie took the book from Austin and began flipping through the pages. Suddenly, the windows in the hallway began to rattle in their metal frames. The floor beneath their feet shook, momentarily knocking the boys off balance. Austin and Charlie looked at each other, both confused and a little scared. Charlie looked down at the book in his hands. It was glowing.

Charlie slammed the book shut, dropped it on the floor, and ran as fast as he could away from the locker. He expected the speedy Austin to run past him, but he never did. Eventually, Charlie stopped running, turned back around, and looked back down the long hallway. Austin was still standing in front of the locker trying to process what had just happened. The rumbling and shaking had stopped when Charlie dropped the book.

"Austin, what the heck was that?" Charlie yelled down the hallway.

"Come back, you scaredy-cat, it stopped," Austin chided his friend. A few moments later Charlie was back by Austin's side in front of the locker again.

"Okay, it stopped. But what was it?" Charlie questioned.

"I have no idea, but that was cool. Do you think it had something to do with the locker?" The book was still lying on the floor, and Charlie bent down and picked it up again.

"It seems like it started when I opened the book and stopped when I dropped it. Let's see if it happens again." Slowly, Charlie opened the book again, this time to a picture of George Washington in a boat crossing an icy river. He recognized it immediately as *Washington Crossing the Delaware*, a famous painting by Emanuel Leutze.

Once again, the boys heard a rumbling sound, and the ground beneath them began to shake. They looked at each other nervously, but neither one ran away. This time they realized that the sound was coming from the locker. Suddenly, the book began glowing in Charlie's hands again. The boys looked at each other, more frightened this time. They watched in shock as the back wall of the locker seemed to dissolve away into nothingness, replaced by a swirling mass of what looked like stars. Stunned, it took Charlie a few moments to realize what it reminded him of. It looked like pictures he'd seen in science class of the swirling Milky Way Galaxy. Charlie looked away from the locker long enough to see that Austin was just as amazed as he was. Both boys' eyes were as wide as saucers.

"Austin, are you seeing this?" Charlie asked his friend, not trusting his own eyes. "What happened to the locker? What's that swirly thing?"

After another moment, the center of the swirl slowly began to open. At first, it was just blackness inside. Then, the boys began seeing images in the darkness. As the center of the swirl grew larger, the image that appeared to them looked like a wide field covered in snow. At the far end of the field was a river, and next to the river was a camp with dozens of tents. In another field they saw men marching in formation. It looked to Austin like they were wearing some sort of military uniform.

Charlie looked closer at the distant images they were seeing in the swirling mass and realized that they weren't just pictures. They were moving. He could see an officer giving orders to some soldiers while several others rode past on horseback.

"Maybe the book is like an old-time movie projector or something," Charlie said to Austin. He didn't really believe it, but his mind was trying to come up with something rational to explain what he was seeing.

Suddenly, Austin took a step forward toward the locker, reached into it with his right arm, and touched the swirling mass where the back wall of the locker used to be. When his fingers touched it, the images pressed backward slightly, as if he were touching plastic wrap on a bowl. When he pressed a little harder, his fingers seemed to break through, sending little ripples through the image, as if he had put his hand in water. Without any fear, Austin pushed his hand further into the swirling mass. When he was up to his elbow, he turned around and looked at Charlie. Charlie's face was pale, like he'd just seen a ghost.

"I think it's a portal. Like a vortex or something." Austin said. He withdrew his arm from the locker and wiggled his fingers. All five fingers were still there.

Charlie, who had finally overcome his initial shock, said to Austin,

"What does it feel like in there? Can you feel anything on the other side?"

"No, I didn't feel anything. It just felt like air. The air was cold. I'm going to stick my head in." Before Charlie could object, Austin moved his body closer to the locker and grabbed the sides with both hands. He lowered his shoulders and stuck his head into the locker and through the portal until his head and shoulders disappeared. After a few moments, Austin withdrew his head from the locker and looked at Charlie. There was a huge smile on Austin's face.

"What? What happened?" Charlie asked eagerly.

"You've got to see for yourself. Check it out." Charlie thought about it a moment, then handed the still-glowing book to Austin, making sure to keep it open to the same page. If Austin could stick his whole head in there and be alright, he figured it would be okay for him, too. Charlie moved forward to the locker and placed his hands on the sides, just as he had seen Austin do. He took one last look at Austin, who was nodding encouragement. Charlie shrugged his shoulders and plunged his head into the portal. After almost two full minutes, Charlie finally pulled back away from the portal. He looked at his friend.

"How can this be real?" Charlie asked incredulously. "I just stuck my head into a portal, and I was in another world. I can't believe it."

Chapter Three

"No. Absolutely not. You're crazy, we can't go through that thing." Even as he said it, Charlie's mind wandered to what was on the other side of that portal. Did it have something to do with the picture of George Washington? When he was nine years old, Charlie had made a list of historical figures he would like to meet. His list read:

George Washington
Theodore Roosevelt
Babe Ruth
Abraham Lincoln
Alexander the Great

Austin could not take his eyes off the portal. Finally, he looked down at the glowing book in his hands, open to the page with Washington crossing the icy Delaware River. Austin wasn't a fan of history the way Charlie was. What he was interested in was an adventure. He looked once more at the portal, then back to Charlie. Then, Austin started climbing into the locker.

"Wait a minute, will you!" Charlie yelled at his best friend. "Let's at least think this through." Austin paused in the locker door.

"Does that mean you're coming with me?" Austin asked hopefully.

"Well, I can't let you go by yourself, can I?" Charlie asked rhetorically. "Before we go through that thing, we need to think about how it works. It opened when we opened the book, and the page we opened it to is what showed up in the portal. Hopefully, on the other side, the book still opens the portal. That will be how we get back home."

"Hopefully?" Austin asked.

"Yes, hopefully. We have no idea how it really works or what we should expect. We might not even be able to come back." Charlie said sternly. Austin paused a moment to think about that, and just as quickly brushed it aside.

"This could be the adventure of a lifetime. Are you coming?" Charlie looked at the glowing book in Austin's hands, then looked at the portal.

"Whatever we do, we can't lose that book," he said and nodded to Austin that he was ready to proceed.

Austin went through the portal first, followed closely by Charlie. When they came out on the other side of the portal, Charlie could feel and hear the fresh snow crunch beneath his feet. He immediately felt the bite of a cold breeze blowing across the open field. About a hundred yards to their left was a tree-lined dirt road, and on the other side of the road was a stone farmhouse. In the field in front of them, stretching across a gentle slope leading to the bank of a river, were dozens of white tents. The tents were aligned in straight rows, with large circular fire pits between the rows at regular intervals. Around the fire pits, Austin and Charlie could see men huddled together. Some were cooking food over the flames; others were warming themselves or drying wet clothes. In the distance, in another field, the boys could see and just barely hear men marching in time together to the beat of a drum.

Behind them, the locker, the hallway, and the entire school were all gone. All that was left was the portal that they had just stepped through. It was an oval shape, and semi-transparent, hanging in the cold air. The boys could see the snowy field behind the portal, which looked like wavy ripples suspended in mid-air. Austin walked back toward the portal with the book still glowing in his hands. He closed the book, and the portal vanished. He walked through the space where the portal was a moment ago, but nothing happened. The book had also stopped glowing when he closed it. Austin looked at his friend.

"Cross your fingers," he said, and opened the book again, flipping through the pages randomly. Nothing happened. Both boys looked at each other nervously. Austin started flipping faster.

"Don't tell me we're stuck here," Austin said, with a little more alarm in his voice than he had planned.

Suddenly, Charlie had an idea. He took the book back from Austin and flipped quickly through the pages until he found the picture of George Washington again. When he opened the book to that page, there was a low rumble, and the book began to glow in his hands again. After a few seconds of rumbling, the portal reappeared, exactly where it was before. Charlie looked at Austin and smiled. He thrust his head into the portal and looked around. With his head through the portal, he could see that he was back inside the locker in their school. Through the open locker door, he could see the hallway and its big glass windows.

"It worked," Charlie said excitedly after he pulled his head out of the portal. "Now we know that we can get back."

"We cannot lose that book," Austin said again, although Charlie didn't need reminding. He handed the book back to Austin, who closed it and held it tightly under his arm. The portal once again disappeared.

Chapter Four

After the excitement of traveling through the portal had worn off, the boys quickly realized that they weren't dressed for this type of weather. They could see their breath, their fingers were turning numb, and both boys had begun to shiver noticeably.

"Let's walk to that farmhouse and see if we can get warm," Charlie suggested. Together, they began walking the hundred yards or so through the freshly fallen snow toward the stone building. As they walked, they talked about the experience they had just shared.

"When we opened the book, it was to the picture of George Washington crossing the Delaware River," Charlie recalled. "When we first looked through the portal, we saw Washington on horseback. Now, we're here. The tents and the river and the snow, it all adds up."

"Adds up to what?" asked Austin. He wasn't quite sure what Charlie was talking about.

"Washington crossed the Delaware River on Christmas Day, 1776," Charlie recalled from one of his history books. "I think the portal took us back in time. If that's correct, that means that the men in those tents are the Continental Army, and that river is the Delaware. We were transported back to December 1776."

"Woah," was all that Austin could muster.

As the boys trudged along through the snow, Charlie filled Austin in on what he could remember about the Revolutionary War. The Continental Army had taken a beating during 1776, culminating in the loss of New York City in the Battle of Long Island, the first major battle after the signing of the Declaration of Independence on July 4th. The defeat in New York was the worst of Washington's military career. Morale amongst the troops was low, and the colonists were at risk of losing the war.

"That's when Washington decided to cross the Delaware River on Christmas Day to launch a surprise attack on Trenton, New Jersey," Charlie told Austin as they got closer to the farmhouse. "Trenton was defended by Hessian troops. Hessians were Germans who sided with England during the Revolution.

"And you think that's what's about to happen here?" asked Austin.

"I don't know for sure, but I think so," Charlie replied. As the boys approached the farmhouse, they noticed two soldiers standing guard outside of the entrance. They looked exactly like the revolutionary soldiers that the boys had seen in their schoolbooks with red, white, and blue uniforms and three-cornered hats.

Before the boys could say anything, one of the soldiers yelled to them,

"You must be the lads that Division sent to us. Hurry now, the Colonel has been waiting for you. He has an important message for you."

The boys looked at each other in shock. How could anyone here be waiting for *them*? Confused, but still freezing cold in the snow, the boys didn't say a word as they followed the soldier into the farmhouse.

Chapter Five

The boys entered the stone farmhouse behind the soldier, thankful to be out of the cold and snow. A fire burned in a large fireplace at one end of the room. In the center of the room was a long wooden table with several maps laid out. Standing over the maps studying them intently was a tall man in an impeccably crisp uniform. The boys could tell by the way the other soldiers deferred to him that this was an important person.

"Colonel Knox," the soldier said, "the messenger boys you were expecting have arrived."

The tall man responded with a booming voice that filled the room.

"Very good. I have an urgent message that must be delivered at once. Can either of you young men read a map?"

The boys stared at him for a few moments, too dumbstruck to speak. Finally, Charlie responded,

"Yes, sir. I can read a map."

"Good, good. Now come over to this table and let me show you where the camps are located."

Colonel Knox proceeded to show Charlie the location of three camps and the best route to reach them. Austin listened as well, but only understood about half of what he was hearing.

"Head east until you reach the river. There you will find the first camp. Find the headquarters tent and deliver one letter to Captain Forrest. Turn north and follow the river for about one mile. There will be another camp. Same as before, deliver one letter to Captain Sargent. Finally, continue north past the second camp another mile and you will reach the third camp. That's Captain Hamilton. Find his tent and give him the final copy." Knox handed Austin a satchel, as Charlie continued to study the map. He looked inside the satchel to find several copies of a letter, each sealed with wax and stamped "HK".

"Once the three messages have been delivered, you are to remain in the service of Captain Hamilton. He is the only commander without a messenger currently. Any questions?" The boys had a million questions, but they slowly shook their heads in unison.

"Go to the kitchen and get a hot meal before you leave. But be quick about it. And see the quartermaster for a coat, or you'll likely freeze to death." Knox dismissed them and went about his business.

The boys left the large main room and entered a smaller room, the kitchen. There was a large black pot warming over a fire in one corner. There were also several big, wooden tables with a few soldiers sitting and eating. The boys found trays on one table and walked to the large pot. They each served themselves a ladle full of something that resembled beef stew. Next to the pot was a basket of biscuits, so each boy took one. They walked to an empty table and sat down by themselves. The quartermaster, having overheard the Colonel, brought the boys two large, wool jackets. They were men's sizes, and nearly reached the boys' feet. They accepted them gratefully.

The boys sat quietly eating. Austin was the first to speak.

"Can you believe this? An hour ago, we were at our school. Now, we're delivering messages for a colonel."

"Not just any colonel," Charlie corrected him. "The soldier called him Colonel Knox. As in Henry Knox."

Austin stared blankly at Charlie, not recognizing the name.

Charlie continued. "Henry Knox was one of George Washington's closest friends and most trusted advisors. After the war, he went on to become our nation's first Secretary of War. Fort Knox is named after him.

"Where they keep the gold?" Austin asked.

"Yes, where they keep the gold, but it's also a military base," Charlie replied. "And you know what else? I'm willing to bet the Captain Hamilton he mentioned is Alexander Hamilton. He and Knox were both artillery officers in Washington's Continental Army.

"I've heard of him," Austin responded. "Isn't he on the ten dollar bill?"

"That's right," Charlie replied. "He's on the ten dollar bill because he went on to become our first Secretary of the Treasury."

Charlie and Austin ate the remainder of their meal in silence, processing what they had been through so far and imagining what was still to come.

Chapter Six

When the boys had finished their meal, they struck out in the cold snow again, this time wearing their oversized jackets, and headed toward the first camp. Austin was carrying the satchel with the three copies of Colonel Knox's message. He had also put the *First Person History* book inside the satchel for safekeeping. Charlie was in front of him with the map that Colonel Knox had given him.

The first camp was easy for them to find. It was the group of tents they had seen just a few hundred yards from where the portal had been. It took them about ten minutes to reach the tents from the stone farmhouse.

Once the boys had entered the encampment, they spotted a few soldiers sitting around a fire pit. As they moved closer to the men, the first thing they noticed was how young they looked. Most of them looked not much older than Austin and Charlie themselves. Although the men had the young faces of teenagers, there was a grizzled hardness to them as well. The young man to Austin's right couldn't have been more than twenty, but his face was dirty and lined with wrinkles.

"Captain Forrest's tent? We have a message for him from Colonel Knox," Austin said to one of the soldiers.

The soldier turned a young but rough-looking face toward the boys, taking them both in with one glance. Without a word, he moved his head in a barely perceptible nod to the left, in the direction of a tent slightly larger than the others, with a flag on a long stick outside of the entrance.

Without another word, the boys left the soldiers and headed toward the tent with the flag.

Charlie was the first to speak this time. "The average age of a revolutionary soldier was between eighteen and twenty years old, with some enlisting as young as fourteen."

"Those guys looked worn out," Austin said of the young soldiers.

"1776 was a tough year of fighting for the Continental Army," Charlie continued. "They took some major defeats, like the Battle of Long Island I told you about earlier. Plus, many of the soldiers' one-year enlistments were about to expire. Food was scarce and the Continental Congress had no way to pay them. The crossing of the Delaware River was a huge risk, but it paid off for Washington, and the victories at Trenton and Princeton turned the tide of the entire war."

"Wow, I didn't know all that," Austin exclaimed. "So, this moment in time is really important for the future of our whole country."

"Extremely," Charlie agreed.

"I guess that means these messages we're delivering are also really important to the future," Austin continued.

"Yeah, I guess you're right," Charlie agreed again. The boys continued toward the tent in silence, both with a newfound sense of purpose.

When they reached the tent with the flag, they stopped and looked at each other. Charlie, unsure of how to proceed, encouraged Austin to make their next move. Austin, without hesitation, pulled back the flap of the tent and called out,

"Captain Forrest? We're messengers sent by Colonel Knox." A friendly voice from within the tent responded to their inquiry.

"Yes, yes, by all means, come right in."

When they entered the tent, it took their eyes a moment to adjust to the darkness from the bright, snowy landscape outside. In front of them stood a man of medium height wearing the gold shoulder epaulets and red waist sash of a Continental officer.

"Welcome, lads. I am Captain Thomas Forrest, Commanding Officer of 2nd Company, Pennsylvania State Artillery. Please tell me, how may I be of service to you?" His friendly manner immediately set the boys at ease.

"Thank you, sir. We have a letter for you from Colonel Knox." Austin reached into the satchel and produced one copy of the letter, handing it to Captain Forrest.

The boys watched the officer intently as he opened the wax-sealed envelope and quickly read the contents. When he finished, he walked over to a small wood-burning stove that was used to warm the tent. He opened a latch on the stove and placed the letter into the flames, where it immediately caught and was quickly reduced to a pile of ashes. Captain Forrest relatched the stove and resumed his place in front of the boys.

"Very good, lads. What were your instructions upon delivery of the letter to my hands?"

Austin answered, "We are supposed to deliver another copy of the letter to Captain Sargent and then one to Captain Hamilton. Then we stay with Captain Hamilton to be his messengers."

"And you know where those gentlemen's camps are located?" This time, Charlie responded.

"Yes, sir. The first camp is about one mile north of here, along the river. The next camp is another mile north, also along the river. Colonel Knox provided us with a map."

"Very good. Stay near to the river and you shan't get lost. If you leave now and don't delay, you shall make your mission before sundown."

Austin, in a sudden burst of patriotism and pride, snapped to attention and gave the captain a crisp hand salute. Charlie, not wanting to appear disrespectful, offered his best salute as well, although Austin had more practice and looked better doing it. Captain Forrest returned their salutes with a smile and a quick salute of his own.

"Very good, lads. Carry on."

Chapter Seven

"That was awesome! I told you this would be an adventure," Austin exclaimed after they had exited the tent. "We're messengers for the Continental Army!" Charlie had a smile on his face as well.

"You're right, this is pretty fun. But we can't forget where we are. We are still kids in the middle of a real war. Once we leave this camp, there could be enemy out there trying to hurt us. We must be extremely careful."

"You're right," said Austin somberly. "So, which way is it to the next camp?" Charlie consulted his map for a moment.

"The river runs north-south and we are on the western side of the river." He looked up from his map and pointed to the river, just past the last row of tents. "If we go left, that's heading north. If we follow the river about one mile in that direction, we should find the next camp."

"Great," Austin said, "Let's get moving. If we keep moving, we won't get too cold." Charlie folded his map and put it into his pocket. Austin threw the satchel over his shoulder and the boys headed out of the camp toward the river. Once they were outside of the camp and within sight of the river, they turned left and began following the river north. After hiking a few hundred yards, the clearing they were in turned into a forest. As they entered the forest, it felt as if they were entering a different world.

"Let's make sure we don't lose sight of that river. If we get lost in these woods we could be in real trouble," Charlie called to Austin, who was a few feet in front of him leading the way.

"Roger that," Austin responded, still enjoying playing the role of a soldier.

The boys were moving a bit slower in the forest than they had been in the clearing, but they were still making good progress. After about thirty minutes of walking, they had worked up a sweat and didn't even feel cold. Before they entered the forest, Charlie had noted that the sun was starting to get lower in the sky. Neither boy had a watch, but Charlie estimated that it was about 4:30 pm. He also figured that they were about halfway to the second camp. If they reached the second camp within the next half hour, they should be able to make it to the third camp before dark, just as Captain Forrest had predicted.

The boys trudged through the snow quietly, and Charlie used the time to reflect on all they had been through that day. Finding the mysterious locker in the even more mysterious hallway at school, opening it to find the strange book that revealed a time portal of some sort, then actually traveling back in time to become messengers for the Continental Army. It still seemed too amazing to believe. He had to admit to himself that although he was scared at first, he was having a great time. It was an adventure, just like Austin said it would be. Charlie was cautious by nature and never took risks if he could avoid them. But this adventure had opened his eyes. Books were great, but experiencing things firsthand was even better.

After a few more minutes of walking, Austin stopped and said,

"I think I see a clearing. Maybe we're at the end of the forest." The boys marched on and soon the forest opened up to a clearing, just like the one they left when they entered the forest. A wide snow-covered field in front of them sloped gently toward the river. Several hundred yards in front of them they could see rows of white tents, arranged nearly identically to the last camp they had just left.

"This must be Captain Sargent's camp. Let's go," Charlie called out as he began running toward the camp. He soon realized he wouldn't be able to run the entire distance and resigned himself to walking quickly. Austin easily caught up to his friend and together they walked the short distance to the encampment.

As they approached the camp from the forest they descended into a slight valley, resulting in the boys having a view of the entire layout of the camp. Austin, using what he had learned from the last camp, spotted one slightly larger tent with a flag posted outside the entrance.

"Look. I bet that's the headquarters tent," he said as he pointed out the flag to Charlie.

"Hey, I bet you're right. You're turning into a real soldier," Charlie complimented his friend. This made Austin beam with pride. As they entered the encampment, they noticed that the faces of the soldiers looked almost identical to the last camp. They were young men but had a hard, haggard look in their eyes. The boys nodded slightly at a group of soldiers they passed. The soldiers barely noticed them.

Austin led them directly to the headquarters tent. They hesitated a moment outside of the tent.

"I wonder what this guy will be like. I hope he's as nice as the last one," Charlie said.

"Only one way to find out," was Austin's reply.

Chapter Eight

Austin announced their presence at the tent in the same manner as he had done previously. "Captain Sargent? We have a message for you from Colonel Knox." This time, the boys were surprised to be greeted by a boy about their own age. He pulled aside the tent flap and invited them inside.

"Captain Sargent is out inspecting the troops. Pleased to wait here until his return, for he is expected shortly."

Austin and Charlie glanced at each other as they followed the boy into the tent. It was furnished in much the same manner as Captain Forrest's tent. A small stove burned in the corner, while the center of the tent was occupied by a map table and some chairs. There were two cots on opposite sides of the tent with wool blankets and small pillows which looked like they were stuffed with hay.

"Are you Captain Sargent's messenger?" Charlie asked the boy.

"Not in an official capacity, although I do deliver messages sometimes. My name is William Howard, and I am Captain Sargent's valet."

Austin looked to Charlie for clarification.

"A valet is like a personal assistant," Charlie said, responding to Austin's look.

"Indeed," William said proudly. "I attend to anything my master needs outside of military matters, such as cleaning and laying out his uniforms, tidying the headquarters tent, and fixing his meals. My mother died when I was young, and my father was killed at Lexington. My aunt took me in, and we became camp followers. Captain Sargent knew my father from our days in Massachusetts. When he saw me outside of his camp one day, he offered me a position as his valet."

"Nice to meet you, William. My name is Austin, and this is Charlie, my best friend. We're…uh…not from around here exactly. We are messengers for Colonel Knox at the moment. Once we have delivered our messages, we're supposed to stay with Captain Hamilton and be his messengers."

"Ahh, Captain Hamilton. A fine officer indeed. You are truly fortunate to be employed in his service." William offered the boys a seat at the map table, which they gladly accepted, their legs being tired after walking from the last camp. William pulled a cot close to the table and sat on it.

"William," Charlie inquired, "how long have you been Captain Sargent's valet?"

"Captain Sargent took me into his service shortly after he took command of the company. That was about four months ago. The original commander of this unit was

Captain Thomas Pierce. Unfortunately, he was wounded at the Battle of Long Island this August past and was unable to continue his service. In his stead, Lieutenant Sargent was given command and promoted to the rank of Captain."

"Wow," was the only response that Charlie could muster. The mention of someone being wounded brought the reality of war back to the forefront of his mind. Next, Austin had a few questions for their new acquaintance.

"Have you been in any battles? Have you been shot at?"

William looked at Austin with an inquisitive smile. "No, there haven't been any battles as of yet, although he tells me that General Washington has something rather large planned for very soon. In any case, I shan't be accompanying him into battle. My duties keep me far away from the fighting."

"Oh," Austin said, a little let down. "One more question."

"By all means," William said, "Ask as many as you like. I am at your service."

"What exactly do messengers do during the fighting?"

"Oh, that is another thing entirely," William responded. "A messenger's first duty is to remain by the side of his commander, making himself available for any messages. You must be there to receive his instructions and transmit his correspondence immediately. The outcome of a skirmish may depend on his orders being communicated to the battlefield rapidly." Austin's eyes lit up at this news. Charlie looked as though he would be sick. They looked at each other but remained silent.

Before they could ask William another question, the tent flap opened and in stepped a man dressed in the same officer's uniform as Captain Forrest, but that's where the similarities ended. This man was short and stout, with a disheveled uniform that was wet from snow and caked with mud. When he entered the tent, William immediately jumped to his feet and stood still with his arms at his sides, what Austin recognized as the Position of Attention. Charlie and Austin saw this and did the same.

"Welcome back, sir. Here are two messengers sent by Colonel Knox with a message for you." With that, William moved to the back of the tent to add more logs to the stove, and Captain Sargent looked at the boys as he removed his uniform jacket.

"Welcome, lads. I am Captain Winthrop Sargent, commander of the Massachusetts Company of Continental Artillery. What do you have for me from Colonel Knox?" Austin quickly retrieved one copy of the letter from his satchel and handed it to the captain. Before opening it, Sargent inspected the seal and turned to address William.

"This might be it, my boy. This might be word of the attack I've told you about." William returned to the center of the tent and waited with Charlie and Austin while Captain Sargent read the letter.

Sargent's countenance went from friendly to serious as he read the letter. When he was finished, he approached the stove and burned the letter in the same fashion as Captain Forrest had done. He returned to where the boys remained standing and again addressed William.

"Well, William my boy. This is it. We are to cross the river tonight and launch a surprise attack on Trenton. You've been a faithful valet, but it's time you assumed more responsibility. I'm hereby promoting you to messenger. You will cross the river tonight by my side. Presently, go and inform the lieutenants and sergeants to report to my tent immediately."

William, a smile on his face, responded with a salute and an enthusiastic *yes, sir!*

After William had departed, Charlie and Austin realized the urgency of delivering the last letter to Captain Hamilton. Charlie addressed Captain Sargent, who was already at his map table making plans.

"I beg your pardon, sir. We have one more copy of this letter to deliver to Captain Hamilton. If you don't require anything further of us, we will be on our way."

"Yes, by all means, go at once. Deliver your message to him with the utmost haste."

Chapter Nine

The boys left the tent quickly, Austin leading the way with Charlie right behind him. Their adrenaline was pumping, both with the importance of delivering their letter and the realization that they would be crossing the river with General Washington tonight. As the boys came within sight of the icy river, they once again turned left to follow it north to Captain Hamilton's camp. They were moving much more quickly than before, alternating between running and walking fast. As they followed the river, there was no forest ahead of them as there had been before. The river had several turns in it, with a few trees lining the banks but not enough to slow their progress. After just a few minutes of traveling, they could even see their destination far off in the distance. The fact that they could see Captain Hamilton's camp made them move even faster. With no forest to slow them down, they covered the distance quickly, taking less than thirty minutes to cover the mile between camps.

When they got to the third and final camp, the setting sun had not yet touched the horizon. They ran through the camp until they found the headquarters tent with a flag posted outside of it. This time, without waiting, they burst into the tent unannounced.

"Captain Hamilton, we have an urgent message for you from Colonel Knox!" Austin shouted as they rushed into the tent. A young man of no more than twenty-one was sitting at the map table in the center of the tent. He wore the same officer's uniform that they had seen twice before, but with his jacket off and shirt sleeves rolled up.

"I'm Captain Hamilton," he stood to address them as they entered the tent. "What news do you bring me?" Austin, without another word, handed him the third and final copy of Colonel Knox's letter. Captain Hamilton perused the letter quickly, his eyes taking in the entirety of the message in just a few moments. After reading the letter, he destroyed it in the same manner as his two fellow officers before him.

"And what of you two?" Hamilton said, addressing the boys. "What's to become of you now that your task is completed? I'm in need of two good messengers to accompany me on this mission, and you seem highly qualified."

Charlie spoke first. "Yes, sir. We were instructed by Colonel Knox to remain with you as your messengers."

"Wonderful. I'm Captain Alexander Hamilton of New York, commander of the New York State Company of Artillery. But you already knew that, apparently. What then are your names, lads?"

"My name is Austin, and this is my best friend Charlie," Austin responded.

"Austin and Charles, splendid. You must be tired after delivering these messages. You're welcome to stay in my tent and rest for a bit. You'll need your strength for what we attempt tonight. I'm off to confer with the officers and NCOs of the company, and to begin preparations for the crossing."

Captain Hamilton donned his uniform jacket and left the tent quickly. They could hear him shouting commands to others as he moved rapidly away from the tent. As they listened to Captain Hamilton's voice fade into the distance, the boys warmed themselves by the stove and discussed all they had experienced thus far.

"We did it," Charlie said. "We delivered our messages to the three camps. We did our part to help the American Revolution. How many kids from our class can say that?"

"And can you believe we will be crossing the river tonight with General George Washington?" Austin added, excitedly.

Charlie looked at his friend. Austin's eyes were glowing. He really did love the adventure that they were on. Charlie had noticed that not only was Austin having a good time but that he was learning a good bit about history as well. But he had something to say that Austin might not like.

"Yea, about that. Austin, listen. That river crossing tonight is going to be very dangerous. And what comes after it will be even more dangerous. A real battle in a real war. You wanted an adventure, and we had one. I was hesitant at first, but I have to admit that this has been fun. But I think we should open the book now and get back home. Back to our own time."

Austin said nothing for a long time. He and Charlie had been best friends for as long as he could remember. Several times, Charlie's quick thinking had gotten them out of tough situations that Austin had gotten them into. He knew that Charlie was right. It *would* be dangerous. But Austin just couldn't bring himself to leave yet.

"You go," Austin finally said. "Thanks for coming this far with me. I can't leave yet. This is the most fun I've ever had. As long as I can remember, I've wanted to be a soldier. I'm sure when we grow up that's what I'll be. You may be a doctor, a scientist, or a historian, but those things sound boring as heck to me. *This* is where I belong." Austin took the *First Person History* book out of his satchel and handed it to Charlie. Charlie looked down at the book in his hands, turning it over and examining it. But he didn't open it. Instead, Charlie set the book on the map table and looked back to Austin.

"If you're staying, then I'm staying too. We've come this far together; I can't leave you now. Besides, your mom would kill me if I came back without you."

Austin smiled a big smile, reached for Charlie, and gave him an awkward hug. Charlie hugged his friend back, but both boys pulled away quickly and acted like it hadn't happened.

"Thanks, pal," Austin said to Charlie. "Now, we should try to get a little rest, like Captain Hamilton said. We might be in for a long night." With that, the boys laid down on the two cots in the small tent and drifted off to sleep.

Chapter Ten

The boys were awakened a few hours later by the sound of Captain Hamilton entering the tent.

"Awaken, lads. The time has come to put our plans into execution. The boats are waiting for us on the riverbank."

As Austin and Charlie rubbed the sleep from their eyes, they saw Captain Hamilton gathering some books and papers from the map table and placing them into a satchel. He handed the satchel to a soldier standing by the entrance of the tent awaiting instructions.

"Take these and place them in my saddlebag, then take my horse to the riverbank to await further instructions. I shall be there shortly."

"Yes, sir," was the soldier's reply, and he quickly left the tent.

The boys exited the tent and found the night air cool and quiet, with light snow beginning to fall. A full moon illuminated the snowy ground so brightly that it looked nearly as bright as daytime. They waited outside the tent for Captain Hamilton to finish gathering his things. Once he exited the tent, the boys walked alongside him as they made their way toward the river. As they walked, Captain Hamilton filled the boys in on some important details that they would need to know in the coming hours. They were to cross the river in a boat with Captain Hamilton and some of his men while his aide, Private Smith (the soldier they saw earlier in the tent) would take his horse across the water on a larger ferry-type boat. After disembarking on the opposite shore, Captain Hamilton would mount his horse and lead the troops on a march to Trenton, a distance of about nine miles. The boys were to stay with Private Smith during the march to Trenton. This being an artillery company, they would stop on a spot of high ground above Queen Street just before they reached Trenton. This would allow them an advantageous position to direct their artillery fire on the Hessians occupying the city.

After a few minutes of walking, the trio reached the river. Standing before them were hundreds of soldiers formed in neatly arranged rows. The boys could see the men shivering in the cold. They looked as though they had been standing there for quite a while, a light dusting of snow had begun to build up on their heads and shoulders. The boys followed Hamilton to the right flank of the formation where his aide, Private Smith, was standing holding the reins of a beautiful white horse. Hamilton spoke to Smith for a moment, then turned back to the boys.

"Charles, Austin, this is Private Smith, my aide. Once we reach the New Jersey shore, you shall meet with Private Smith and take your directions from him. From this moment forward, you are never to leave my side unless directed. The same goes for Private Smith, of which he is already well aware. Take a few moments to get acquainted, we shall begin the crossing shortly."

With that, the boys watched Hamilton walk to the front of the formation and address the large company of soldiers. His speech was spirited and motivational. He told them of the challenges that lay ahead, but also spoke about the glory of the victory that was to follow. His men cheered him wildly and were enthusiastic despite the bitterly cold conditions.

While Hamilton was speaking to his men, Private Smith introduced himself to the boys.

"Good evening, young men. My name is Private Daniel Smith. How long have you been in the service of Captain Hamilton?"

"We just got here today, actually," Austin answered.

"Right into the action, I see. Excellent."

"Private Smith, do you expect there's anybody waiting for us on the other side of the river?" Charlie asked, trying to mask the concern in his voice.

"There's always that possibility. But with this being Christmas night, I expect that the Hessians have no idea we are coming. General Washington has intelligence that the Hessians have no outposts or patrols established tonight. We should be able to take them by surprise."

The boys spoke to Private Smith for a few more minutes, going over the details of where they would meet once they were across the river. Then, as Captain Hamilton wrapped up his speech, Smith took the reins of the horse and led it downstream a few hundred yards where the boys could see in the moonlight other horses and men waiting to board several larger boats.

Hamilton gave one final order to his troops, and they all began moving at once. It appeared to the boys to be chaos, but it was an ordered chaos as well. Every man seemed to know exactly which boat to board. As the first men began boarding the boats and crossing the icy river, the remaining men lined up on the shore awaiting their turn. Each boat could hold about a dozen men, so the boats would be required to make many trips back and forth across the river, ferrying more men across each time.

Hamilton rejoined the boys and pointed to a boat waiting on the shore. A few men were already loaded into the boat, clearly waiting for their commander to join them before shoving off. The trio walked together down to the riverbank, Hamilton leading the way with the boys following close behind. Once they were beside the boat, Austin said quietly to Charlie,

"We're supposed to get in first. The commander is always the last one in and the first one out." Charlie looked at Austin for a moment, then said,

"How do you know that?"

"It's military protocol."

"Okay," Charlie said, deferring to Austin's knowledge of the military. Austin grabbed the side of the boat and hopped over effortlessly. He reached his hand out and helped his friend climb in, a motion they had repeated hundreds of times before, climbing trees and playing on playgrounds together.

Captain Hamilton took one last look at the busy action around him on the Pennsylvania shore before stepping gracefully into the boat. The oarsmen immediately shoved off into the icy water and just like that, Austin and Charlie were crossing the Delaware River on their way to the Battle of Trenton.

Chapter Eleven

Although they were with Alexander Hamilton, not George Washington, the scene before the boys appeared much the same as the famous painting they remembered. Hamilton was not standing, as Washington was in the painting. Instead, he was sitting in the bow of the boat, closely observing the opposite shore and the men disembarking from their boats as quietly as possible in the moonlit darkness. There was also no American flag accompanying them. Charlie did see the colored flag from the headquarters tent in the boat being carried by a very young-looking soldier. Charlie had heard Austin call this flag a guidon. But other than those details, the scene was eerily similar to the painting. Dozens of boats rowed quietly across the icy river just a few yards from one another. In the bow of the boat sitting to the left of Hamilton was a soldier holding a long pole. His job was to push large chunks of ice away from the path of the boat. Every now and then the boys felt a spray of water hit their faces from the slapping of the oars in the water, and the freezing water stung their cheeks. For the most part, however, the boys didn't notice the cold temperature because their bodies were warm with adrenaline.

The boats proceeded slowly but surely across the river, and after about twenty minutes the boys once again planted their feet on dry land, this time on the New Jersey side of the river. All around them, the organized chaos had resumed. Soldiers were disembarking their boats and hurrying to form columns on a wide, snowy path heading south parallel to the river. Further downstream, they could see the horses and heavy artillery cannons being unloaded from the ferry boats.

The boys kept close to Captain Hamilton, as he had instructed. Charlie thought that Hamilton's personality had shifted noticeably since they had landed on the New Jersey shore. Instead of the quiet, reserved young officer they met in the tent, they witnessed Hamilton issuing orders and taking control of the organized chaos around him. He never shouted commands in anger but spoke with authority. He did not belittle his subordinates but spoke to them with respect.

As Hamilton continued supervising the soldiers forming columns on the road, Private Smith walked up leading Hamilton's white horse. Hamilton took the reins from Smith and told him,

"You and the messenger boys shall stay between the first and second columns while we march. Stay alert to any calls for *Messengers forward*. If you hear that, come seek me at once. Keep yourselves safe, for you may be vital to our victory." Smith responded with a salute and quickly led the boys away as Hamilton mounted his horse and moved to the front of the first column of men.

Austin, Charlie, and Private Smith took their positions between the first and second columns of soldiers on the road and within a few minutes, they heard the command *Forward, march*. With that, all the soldiers began moving at once, and the great mass of men moved forward along the snow-covered road. The men moved slowly but steadily, staying quiet for the most part but occasionally the boys could hear muffled conversations between soldiers. The men marched with their muskets slung over their shoulders, content to keep their bodies warm through movement. Charlie looked up at the sky and saw the full moon directly overhead. He guessed that it was around midnight.

"I wonder how long it will take to march nine miles," he wondered out loud to Austin.

"I don't know," Austin replied, "but probably a few hours. I bet we will make it before morning. That would be the best time for a sneak attack." The boys marched on, taking in the sights and sounds. They could see Captain Hamilton at the front of the first column of men on his white horse. He looked majestic in his crisp officer's uniform on the beautiful horse in the light of the full moon.

After several hours of marching, the boys were becoming exhausted. They weren't used to this kind of physical activity or staying up all night long. Private

Smith must have seen their exhaustion because he assured them,

"Not much further, boys. Less than an hour remaining, I'd say."

Sure enough, after less than an hour more of marching, the boys saw Hamilton direct the column off the main road and to the left, in the direction of a low hill. As the columns of marching men veered to the left, the boys could see the beginning of daylight forming in the eastern sky.

Suddenly, Charlie looked at Austin with a look of terror on his face. Austin looked around to find the source of Charlie's fear but couldn't find anything.

"What is it?" Austin asked, confused.

"Where's your satchel?" Charlie asked urgently.

"The book!" Austin looked everywhere around him frantically but knew immediately that it was hopeless. He hadn't had the satchel with him since they left the tent. The book was gone.

Chapter Twelve

Austin was almost in tears as the boys marched up the low hill with the rest of the columns. "I can't believe I left it," he said over and over again.

"Let's think back to the last time we had it. Do you remember when that was?" Charlie tried to console his friend, but inside he felt both upset and afraid. Without that book, there was no way they could get home again.

"We were in Captain Hamilton's tent. We were talking about leaving. I handed you the book, but you decided to stay." Austin looked at Charlie, whose face started turning red. He looked away from Austin when their eyes met. "Wait," Austin said, "What did you do with the book after I handed it to you?" It was Charlie's turn to almost cry.

"Oh boy. I set it on the map table and forgot to pick it up again."

"What happened after that? I don't remember," Austin asked his friend.

"Let's think," Charlie said. "After Captain Hamilton woke us up, we left the tent and walked with him to the river."

"Before we left the tent, there was another soldier waiting for orders from Captain Hamilton," Charlie recalled. "Hamilton handed the soldier something and he left the tent quickly. What was it that he handed the soldier?"

Austin's face brightened momentarily. "It was my satchel. He was putting maps and documents from the map table into it. He must have picked up our book and put it into the satchel."

"Let's hope so," Charlie replied. "He handed the satchel to Private Smith and told him to put it in his horse's saddlebag." Charlie looked to the front of the formation that had now stopped marching on top of the low hill. He saw Hamilton and noticed the two saddlebags hanging over the haunches of his brilliant white horse. "If we're lucky, our book is right up there with Captain Hamilton."

"I sure hope so," Austin said. "I'm having fun, but I don't want to be stuck here forever. I'm starting to miss my family." Charlie was missing his family, too. He was ready to go home.

"We have to get into those saddlebags. Maybe Private Smith can help us."

Chapter Thirteen

The boys never took their eyes off Captain Hamilton and his horse. They watched as he instructed his men to position their artillery pieces and prepare their ammunition. As the soldiers worked, Private Smith approached the boys.

"Come, young gentlemen. Captain Hamilton has a mission for you." The boys looked at each other. Charlie was the first to speak.

"We actually had a favor to ask of you," he said meekly.

"Come along, don't keep the captain waiting," was the terse reply they received. As they hurried to Captain Hamilton's position, they exchanged glances again.

When they reached Captain Hamilton's location, they were surprised to see another face they recognized standing with him. Standing next to the short and slender Hamilton was the tall and powerful frame of Colonel Henry Knox, whom they'd met earlier in the stone farmhouse. He looked like a giant standing next to Captain Hamilton.

"Good morning lads," Knox said as a predawn orange glow began to spread over the horizon to the east. "It seems as though you delivered my messages successfully, for here we all stand in New Jersey." Tall Austin and short Charlie standing together in front of tall Knox and short Hamilton must have felt like they were looking into the future when they were actually staring into the past.

Hamilton spoke next. "Charles, I need you to go to General Washington's position and inform him that we are ready to commence our barrage. He will be on the road to the north of us with Major General Greene's division of infantry."

With the mention of George Washington, Charlie momentarily forgot the problem of the missing book.

"Yes, sir!" he responded enthusiastically. He looked in the direction that Hamilton had pointed and in the slowly growing daylight he could just barely make out a large mass of soldiers formed on the road about half a mile away.

"Excuse me, sir. You don't want us to go together?" Austin asked Captain Hamilton.

"No, young man. I need you to remain here with me, should the battle commence before Charles' return."

Austin and Charlie looked nervously at each other. Since they had crossed through the portal, they had always been together. The thought of being apart from each other in this strange place made them both more than a little scared.

Once the officers had moved on to other matters, Charlie and Austin spoke quietly to each other. Charlie was the first to speak.

"Okay, I guess I have to go find General Washington. I wish you were going with me. But while I'm gone you need to get our book back."

"I will," was Austin's reply, although he didn't think he sounded very confident.

Chapter Fourteen

Charlie started running in the direction Captain Hamilton had pointed, toward the formation of men on the road to the north. As he was running, several different thoughts were running through his mind. He was excited at the prospect of actually meeting George Washington, something that seemed unfathomable just a day ago. He also thought about how he had misplaced the book. He still felt terrible about it, and he hoped that Austin would be able to get it back. As he alternately ran and walked fast across the predawn New Jersey countryside, a new thought popped into his head. He was alone on a battlefield just a few hundred yards away from the enemy army. This thought made him redouble his efforts and run faster toward the relative safety of the Continental Army in front of him.

After about ten minutes of running and walking fast, Charlie began to approach the infantrymen in formation on the road outside of Trenton. He could see individual soldiers now, whereas they had appeared to him as a mass of bodies before. As he approached them, he wondered how he would identify himself. He didn't have to wonder for long. As he approached the formation, a soldier with upside down stripes on his sleeve directed him to stop.

"Stop. Announce yourself. What are you doing here, boy?" the sergeant barked at him. Charlie, his heart pounding from the running but also because he was nervous, said in a firm voice,

"I'm a messenger for Colonel Knox with a message for General Washington."

"Aye. The general is up front, on his horse. You shan't miss him. Hurry along now." With that, Charlie ran quickly to the front of the formation, past row upon row of young men in their mismatched uniforms with their muskets unslung, held in their hands and ready to attack.

When he finally reached the front of the long formation of soldiers, Charlie spied two men on horseback. One of them he didn't recognize, but Charlie guessed that this was probably Major General Nathanael Greene. Greene was one of Washington's division commanders, and also one of his favorite comrades-in-arms. The other man on horseback was immediately recognizable to Charlie from the pictures he had seen in school textbooks. The white hair under the big tri-corner hat, the impeccably crisp uniform with the powder blue sash. There was no doubt in his mind that he was looking at General George Washington.

Charlie knew from his reading that during the war and during his presidency, Washington was addressed by others as "Your Excellency." Washington himself didn't like the title, but it stuck. Charlie, summoning all of his courage, approached the two men on horseback. In his strongest voice he announced,

"Excuse me, Your Excellency. I've just come from Colonel Knox with a message for you." Washington paused his conversation with Greene mid-sentence and looked down at Charlie. He was an exceptionally tall man by 18th century standards, standing at least six feet, two inches tall. Atop his horse staring down at the diminutive 11-year-old, Washington looked to Charlie like the mountain in South Dakota that would later bear his image.

In a booming voice that seemed to carry across the predawn countryside, Washington replied,

"Yes, my son. What is the message?"

"Colonel Knox reports that they are in position and ready to begin their barrage, Your Excellency."

"Thank you, my son," was his response. Then, turning to Greene again, Washington said, "I have every confidence in you and your men, old friend. I will observe the battle from Colonel Knox's position on the hill. Once his artillery barrage is complete, lead your men into the city. Our victory will be swift." Greene said farewell to his Commander-in-Chief and returned to his men. Washington then turned his attention back to Charlie.

"Shall I give you a ride back? It's a dreadfully long way to run, as you already know." Washington reached out his hand and held it toward Charlie, offering to help him up onto his horse. Charlie was momentarily stunned by the offer but recovered quickly and took General Washington's outstretched hand. Washington's large hand lifted him effortlessly into the air and deposited him on top of the horse behind his back. This was Charlie's first time on horseback, and a moment he would remember forever.

Washington kicked his horse with his heels, and it began galloping. Charlie didn't want to fall off, so he wrapped his arms around Washington's waist.

I can't believe I'm hugging George Washington, he thought to himself as they rode quickly back toward Colonel Knox and Captain Hamilton.

Chapter Fifteen

After Charlie had left, Austin turned his attention toward retrieving the *First Person History* book. Hamilton and Knox had ridden off together to inspect some artillery emplacements, and Austin figured that Private Smith was his best bet at getting the book back. He saw Private Smith walking behind Hamilton and Knox, remaining out of the way yet available should his commander need anything. Austin walked up to where Private Smith was and fell in step with him. He knew he had to be careful about what he said next. He also knew he had to act fast, because there would be no chance to get the book back once the fighting started.

"How many Hessians do you think are in the town?" he asked, trying to sound nonchalant.

"Captain Hamilton said that the latest report was around 1,500 Hessians," Smith responded. "It's also reported that they were celebrating Christmas well into the night, and that they have no idea we are approaching."

"That should make it easy for us to take them by surprise," Austin responded, keeping the conversation casual while still looking for a way to mention the book.

The two walked slowly behind Hamilton and Knox as they made their final preparations for the upcoming battle. Austin finally decided to go for it.

"Remember before we crossed the river, when you came into Captain Hamilton's tent, and he gave you a satchel to take to his horse?" Austin held his breath as he watched Private Smith for a reaction.

"Indeed, I remember. I believe I saw you and your friend Charles in the tent as well." Austin thought this was a good sign and kept going.

"That's right, we were there resting after delivering Colonel Knox's message to three different camps. Anyway, the satchel Captain Hamilton gave you was mine, and he accidentally picked up a book that belonged to me. I had left it on his map table when I fell asleep."

"Well, if that's the case, I can retrieve it for you from Captain Hamilton's saddlebag. What's so special about the book?"

Austin had anticipated this question and had a response ready. "It's a book my mother gave me before I left to follow the soldiers," he said. Austin didn't like lying, but he couldn't let Smith know the truth about the book. "Please, whatever you do, don't open the book. It's very personal to me, and I would ask that you respect my privacy."

"Of course. I'll retrieve it at my first opportunity," Private Smith responded. This was going better than Austin could have hoped.

As Austin watched Hamilton and Knox ride along the artillery line with Private Smith following them, he felt as though he had done as much as he could at the moment to get the book back. He glanced in the direction that Charlie had run off on his mission and, if he squinted in the hazy dawn, could just barely make out a horse and rider approaching the hill they were on. He kept watching the figure on horseback as he approached. He could make out a tall man in a military uniform. Then, Austin realized at once that the figure was George Washington. At the same time he realized this, he noticed that there was another person on the horse with Washington, a much smaller person. Austin recognized his best friend, Charlie, holding tight around Washington's waist as his horse galloped ever closer.

Chapter Sixteen

Charlie felt like a conquering hero riding up the hill on the back of a horse with George Washington, one of the greatest generals in history. As they reached the crest of the hill, Charlie could see Hamilton and Knox approaching their Commander-in-Chief. He also saw Austin running toward him. Austin reached out his hand to help his friend down, but he couldn't stop staring at Washington. Reunited with his friend, the only thing Charlie could manage to say was,

"I just rode on a horse with George Washington."

"That's amazing. You'll have one heck of a story to tell when we get home," Austin replied. "Speaking of getting home, I talked with Private Smith about getting our book back. He said he would get it back for us."

"That's great!" Charlie exclaimed. Almost simultaneously, they both started looking around to find Private Smith. They spotted him standing just to the right of Captain Hamilton's horse, looking up at him as if about to speak. The boys, who were close enough to see what was happening but outside of earshot, glanced hopefully at each other.

"He must be about to ask Captain Hamilton for the book," Austin said to Charlie, who nodded in agreement. The boys continued to watch the interaction closely. Private Smith got Captain Hamilton's attention, who in turn leaned forward slightly to better hear his aide's request. After Smith had said a few words, the boys saw Hamilton nodding in assent at whatever Smith had asked and return his attention to Washington. They then saw Smith reach into Captain Hamilton's saddlebag, rummage around inside for a moment, then withdraw the satchel. From the satchel he withdrew their book, *First Person History*. The boys nearly squealed with delight and ran toward Private Smith, who turned to them as they approached.

"Is this the book you were referring to?" Smith asked Austin.

"Yes! Thank you for helping us retrieve it," Austin replied as he reached anxiously for the satchel and book. Private Smith handed them to him and then, looking at Charlie said,

"You seem rather excited that Austin has gotten his book back." Charlie, surprised, said coyly,

"I-I just know how much the book means to him."

"A true friend indeed," Private Smith replied and with that, returned to his duties.

Chapter Seventeen

The boys hardly had time to celebrate their reunion with the book before they heard Washington giving orders to Hamilton to begin the attack.

"General Greene and his men are in position and stand ready to assault the city. Captain Hamilton, give your men the order to begin shelling the Hessian positions. Continue the barrage for 20 minutes. Upon your ceasefire, General Greene and his men will take the city by storm."

"Yes, Your Excellency," was Hamilton's response, as he rode toward his artillery positions. Not wanting to miss the start of one of the greatest battles in American history, the boys ran quickly to catch up with him. They reached his position at the center of the artillery formation just as he was addressing his troops.

"On my signal, men, commence firing," Hamilton said, raising his gleaming saber above his head. For a moment, every soldier's eyes were fixed on their captain. With one smooth motion, he sliced downward with his saber and yelled, "Fire!"

The boys clasped their hands over their ears, expecting every cannon to fire simultaneously. That wasn't the case, however. The cannons were paired, so that half of the cannons were ready to fire while the other half were reloading. This technique reduced the time between volleys and also conserved ammunition.

The concussion from the artillery fire was deafening, even with their ears covered and only half of the cannons firing. The boys instinctively laid down on the ground to reduce their silhouette. They were positioned well behind the firing line, not wanting to be in anybody's way. From where they were on the backside of the hill, they could see the cannons firing but not where their rounds were landing. They watched Captain Hamilton as he rode along the firing line checking on his troops. Occasionally he would give them some words of encouragement or direction, but for the most part he just watched as they kept up the steady barrage of artillery fire.

"We must have really taken the Hessians by surprise," Austin yelled to Charlie through the roar of the cannons. "It's been about ten minutes and I don't think they've even returned fire yet." As soon as he had finished his sentence, the boys were shaken by a massive explosion about 50 yards away from them. The ground shook, and dirt and debris landed all around where they were lying. Luckily, the round had landed behind the artillery line and none of the soldiers were injured. Austin, realizing that they could be in real danger, scanned the area quickly for a more protected location. He spotted a large fallen tree about a dozen yards from them and pointed for Charlie to run to it.

"Get behind the tree!" he said as they were running, "It will give us better cover from any more incoming rounds." They reached the downed tree and threw themselves behind its massive trunk just as another Hessian round exploded beside them.

"That one hit right where we were before," Austin said, still catching his breath. "If we hadn't moved, we'd be in a million pieces right now."

Over the next ten minutes, the boys watched as several more explosions rocked the area on the hill where the Continental artillery was positioned. They stayed behind the trunk of the fallen tree and kept their heads down. Suddenly, they noticed that all of Hamilton's artillery went silent. They peeked over the edge of the tree and saw Captain Hamilton riding his horse back and forth along the line of cannons giving his men the command to cease fire.

"The barrage is over," Austin said to Charlie. "General Greene's infantry should be starting their assault on the Hessians in the city right now." Austin looked closely at his friend for the first time since the fighting had begun. Charlie looked pale and terrified.

"Hey, we're going to be fine," Austin said to reassure his friend. "The worst of it for us is over now. With the assault beginning, the Hessians will focus their attacks on the infantry. We should be safe up here on the hill now."

Slowly, the boys crept forward toward the line of now-silent cannons. With the infantry attack under way, the artillery hill was a fairly safe place to watch the action. The boys stood near Captain Hamilton and Private Smith, who were both observing the battlefield closely. Occasionally, Smith would point out something significant to the boys.

"There is General Washington," he said, pointing to a figure on horseback. Washington was just behind the front line of General Greene's infantrymen, motivating them and giving occasional directions. As the infantry moved from street to street, it was clear that the attack was going well. The Continentals looked organized and aggressive, while the Hessians were unorganized and slow in reacting to the surprise attack.

After about an hour of intense fighting in the town, it was clear that the Hessians were defeated. Scared Hessian soldiers began to break ranks and retreat, which made the attacking Continental infantry even more effective. Soon, the boys saw Generals Greene and Washington riding back toward the artillery hill. Colonel Knox and Captain Hamilton greeted them enthusiastically.

"A resounding victory!" Knox exclaimed when Washington was within earshot.

"Yes," the Commander-in-Chief responded. "Our men fought extremely well. Our surprise strategy was the key to this much needed victory. But it was a hard-earned victory. Our men are exhausted. We need to decide what our next move shall be."

Austin and Charlie listened intently as Washington's officers shared their opinions on what to do next.

"We have them on the run," Hamilton insisted. "We should pursue the fleeing Hessians and wipe them out." General Greene was a bit more cautious.

"The few that retreated do not pose a threat. Our men need time to recover. We should set up a garrison in the city of Trenton while we plan our next attack." Washington listened carefully to the opinions of his fellow officers. After they all had a chance to speak, he addressed them with authority and finality.

"Our men fought bravely today. They did everything we asked of them without complaint. The army is in no condition to continue fighting without proper rest. We will march our army back across the river to our camp of the previous night. There we will allow the men to rest while we plan our next move. Colonel Knox, you are in charge of the prisoners. See that they are escorted back across the river safely. They are to be treated with respect at all times. Captain Hamilton, see that all of the captured provisions from Trenton are collected and brought back to camp with us. Muskets, ammunition, food, and warm clothing are of the utmost priority."

With that, the officers dispersed to inform their men of the new plans. Austin and Charlie followed Private Smith back to Captain Hamilton's company of men. The men were already forming themselves into squads and platoons and beginning to move the big artillery cannons back to the road.

Chapter Eighteen

The march back to the boats was uneventful. The troops were tired but in good spirits from the overwhelming victory. They kept up a light chatter as they marched briskly through the snowy countryside. Charlie took this opportunity to give Austin another history lesson.

"A few days after the Battle of Trenton, Washington's army got another decisive victory at the Battle of Princeton. Confidence was high going into 1777. Without the victories at Trenton and Princeton, I'm not sure we would have won the war. There might never have been a United States of America."

"It's crazy to think that we played some small role in that," Austin said.

"It really is," replied Charlie. "What if we hadn't been able to get the messages to the captains? Would the history we know have changed? Would the world we go back to be completely different?" Neither of them wanted to ponder that question, so they let it drop.

By the time they got back to camp, it was well after dark. The adrenaline from the battle had sustained the boys through the long foot march and river crossing, but as they approached the long rows of white tents, they suddenly felt exhausted. After several unsuccessful attempts, they finally located Captain Hamilton's command tent where they had gotten a few hours' sleep before crossing the river the first time.

"I don't think I've ever been so tired," Charlie said as they collapsed onto their cots. It just occurred to him that they hadn't slept in over 24 hours. "This has been the adventure of a lifetime. I can't believe all the things we've experienced. Meeting great men like George Washington and Alexander Hamilton. Delivering messages for Henry Knox. Crossing the Delaware River at night, just like we learned about in history class. And witnessing the Battle of Trenton up close. I never could have imagined doing anything so terrifying just a few days ago."

Austin looked at his friend and nodded. He took his satchel off and withdrew the *First Person History* book, turning it over in his hands but not daring to open it yet.

"It has been pretty amazing," he said. "But we should really think about getting home. We didn't make it home last night, our families must be worried sick about us."

Charlie thought about that for a moment. "I read a story about time travel once that was similar to our situation here. When the character went through the time portal, time in their world stopped. That means that when they returned, it was like they hadn't been gone at all. I don't know if that will happen for us or not. But anyway, I agree with you. Let's leave here first thing tomorrow morning."

The boys awoke to the sound of Reveille being played on a bugle. A light snow was falling again as they exited the tent. Around them, soldiers moved quickly, all seemingly headed in the same direction. They were assembling in the field near the river where they had held formation before the river crossing.

"This might be our chance to open the book and get home," Charlie said to Austin as the soldiers hurried past them. But before they could act on that idea, Private Smith came around the corner of the tent looking for them.

"Hurry gents, you won't want to miss this formation. You've been recommended for an award." The boys looked at each other, astonished, then quickly followed Private Smith to the assembly area.

When the boys reached the clearing, they found the entire company of soldiers lined up in formation just as they had been before the crossing when Captain Hamilton gave them his pep talk. They took their informal place beside Private Smith at the right of the formation. At the front, the boys could see Washington, Knox, and Hamilton flanked by several rows of enlisted men standing side by side.

"For unwavering bravery in battle, I'm pleased to award these soldiers the Continental Star." Washington's booming voice carried easily over the snowy field. He walked down the rows of soldiers, pinning a small gold star on each young man's uniform collar. The men stood perfectly still with their arms by their side, at the Position of Attention. After Washington had placed the star on their collar, each man presented him with a hand salute. Washington returned the salute and smiled before moving on to the next soldier.

After every soldier had been recognized, Washington turned to Colonel Knox.

"I believe we have just two more awards to be given, is that correct?"

"Yes, Your Excellency," Knox responded, and turned to look at Captain Hamilton. Without a word, Hamilton signaled to Private Smith.

"That's you. Hurry to the front. Don't keep the general waiting." The boys looked nervously at each other but jogged quickly to the front of the formation. They stood side by side, between Hamilton and Knox, facing the company of Continental Army soldiers. Knox was the first to speak.

"These young messengers came to us just a few days ago and were immediately given the critical task of distributing the river crossing orders throughout the Regiment. Without hesitation, they braved unknown dangers to accomplish their task with the required urgency. Because of their diligence, the river crossing was a success, leading to a successful surprise attack and a complete and total victory over the Hessians. The crossing of the river would not have been successful without the efforts of these young messengers."

Next, General Washington stood in front of them and addressed the formation of soldiers.

"For conspicuous honor, fidelity, and bravery in the face of danger. For accomplishment of their mission above and beyond the call of duty, I award these two young men the Continental Star." Washington turned to face Austin, pinning the star on his shirt. "On behalf of the Continental Congress, The Continental Army, and myself, thank you for your service to the cause of liberty." Austin summoned all the faux military bearing he could muster, snapped off a crisp salute, and nearly shouted,

"Thank you, SIR!" Washington smiled, returned his salute, and said,

"You'll make a fine soldier one day."

Next, Washington took a few steps to his right until he was standing in front of Charlie. The tall man leaned forward to get a better look at the diminutive boy and said,

"Ahh, yes. My riding companion. Keep at it, and you shall make a fine horseman one day." Washington winked at Charlie and pinned the gold star on his shirt. Charlie, looking almost straight up, gave his best salute and responded with,

"Thank you, Your Excellency."

Chapter Nineteen

Half an hour later, the boys were standing alone in the snowy field near the stone farmhouse, just about where they had been when they came through the portal. They both still had their gold stars affixed to their shirts, too proud to remove them just yet. Austin withdrew the *First Person History* book from his satchel and handed it to Charlie.

"Are you ready?" Charlie asked, although he already knew the answer.

"Ready," Austin replied. Even though they had tested the portal and were relatively sure they could get back, they were both still a little nervous and ready to be home. Charlie opened the book and waited for the rumbling to begin.

It didn't.

Charlie turned as white as a ghost. He looked down at the book in his hands and then back up at Austin.

"Remember," Austin said to his friend reassuringly, "It has to be open to the page of George Washington."

"Oh yeah!" Charlie said as he let out a deep sigh of relief, the color returning to his face. "Boy, I really gave myself a scare." Charlie flipped through the pages of the book until he came to the familiar face of George

Washington. Immediately, the book began to glow in his hands, and he could hear and feel a low rumble around them getting louder and louder. Suddenly, the air around them started to move in a wavy motion, like heat waves. The waves turned into swirls as the portal began to open. A few moments later they were staring through the portal into the hallway of their school. They could see the large, old windows directly across the hallway from the locker where they found the book. The portal hung in midair about a foot off the ground and about five feet tall, exactly the height of the locker.

Charlie, still holding the book open to Washington's page, motioned for Austin to go first. Austin slowly stuck his arm into the portal, leaning into the swirling mass until it reached his shoulder. He turned back to take one last look at the snowy field and the year 1776. Then, with one motion, Austin hopped through the portal and emerged standing in the school hallway. He turned to face the row of lockers and could see Charlie looking at him through the portal at the back of the open locker.

"It worked! Come on through," Austin yelled into the locker, not sure if Charlie would even be able to hear him. He reached his arm into the locker, through the portal, and held out his hand for his friend to take. Charlie could see Austin on the other side of the portal and saw him reach his arm back through. He took one last look around him and grabbed Austin's hand with his right hand, holding tight to the book with his left. He stepped into the portal and emerged back in the hallway with Austin.

Austin and Charlie didn't say anything for a while. They just stood there looking at the portal and the glowing book in Charlie's hands. After about a minute, Charlie looked at Austin. Austin nodded in unspoken agreement, and Charlie closed the *First Person History* book. As quickly as it had begun, the rumbling stopped and the portal disappeared, leaving the locker normal once again. Austin closed the locker and placed the lock back in the handle, making sure to leave it unlocked. He replaced the yellow caution tape as well as he could, then stepped back to stand beside Charlie.

"Let's go home," he said.

Chapter Twenty

They walked home in silence. Austin carried the satchel Colonel Knox had given him with the *First Person History* book still inside. Charlie had removed his gold star medal and held it in his hand, staring at it in disbelief. After a few minutes, they came to the intersection where their paths home split. Austin lived three houses down the street to the left, and Charlie lived two houses down on the right. The streetlights were beginning to flicker on.

Neither boy seemed to know what to say in the moment, so they just stood there in the fading daylight for a while, thinking about all they had experienced. Finally, Charlie broke the silence.

"Listen, let's not tell anyone about this. At least not yet." Austin had already thought about this on the walk home and agreed.

"Right," he said. "I'll hide the book when I get home." Austin looked down at the ground, then back at Charlie. He spoke hesitantly. "You know, there are a lot more pages in this book. Now that we know how it works, we could be better prepared if we wanted to explore another page." Charlie gave Austin a stern look, then his face broke into a huge smile.

"Just promise you won't go without me."

"Deal!" Austin said, laughing. They high fived each other before turning in opposite directions toward their homes.

Chapter Twenty One

His mother was washing dishes in the kitchen when Charlie walked through his front door.

"Hi, dear," his mother said casually. "Where have you been, it's after eight o'clock?"

"Oh, uh, one of my friends wanted some extra help with a history test coming up, so we were at the park studying."

"That's so sweet of you, dear," his mother said. "You're such a good friend." Charlie smiled sheepishly, turned toward the stairs, and raced up to his bedroom. When he got there, he dug through the mess of clothes in his closet, finally withdrawing an old shoe box. Sitting on his bed, he examined the contents of the box. A Mike Trout rookie card in a protective plastic sleeve. Some cool rocks and bird feathers he had collected over the years. A few other random items that were meaningful to a boy of eleven. He reached into his pocket and withdrew the Continental Star he had been awarded by General George Washington. He placed the star in the box, took one last, long look at it, and placed the box back in his closet.

When Austin got home, his father was sitting on the couch watching the evening news.

"Hiya, champ," his father said to him. "Where have you been?"

"Hi dad. I stayed late after school to shoot some hoops. Basketball tryouts are in a few weeks."

"That's my boy," his father said proudly. Austin took the stairs two at a time as he climbed toward his bedroom. Inside the sanctuary of his room, he withdrew the *First Person History* book from the satchel. He held it in his hands for a long time, examining the outside closely. It looked just like any other old book. But Austin knew now what this book could do. He walked to the bookshelf under the window in his bedroom. Most of his books were about sports stars and military stories. He figured the best place to hide a book was in plain sight surrounded by other books. So, he found an empty spot on his bookshelf and slid the *First Person History* book into its new home, between *Bo Knows Bo* and *Red Badge of Courage*. Next, he walked to his dresser, where he had a cork board hanging on the wall. Pinned to his board was a picture of his grandfather in a military uniform. Pinned next to the photo was his grandfather's Purple Heart Medal. Austin took the Continental Star out of his pocket and pinned it next to the photo.

"For you, Grandpa."

www.ingramcontent.com/pod-product-compliance
Lightning Source LLC
LaVergne TN
LVHW042156070526
838201LV00047BA/1428